Jetsons On The Move

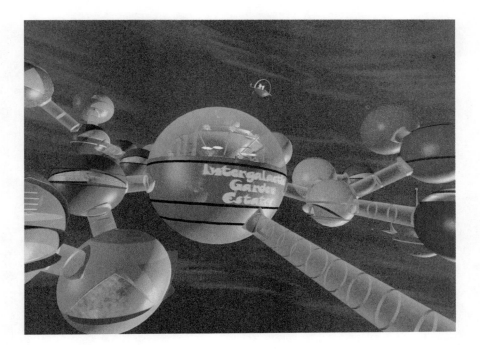

Adapted by Marc Gave

Based on a screenplay by Dennis Marks

Illustrated with full-color photographs from the film

Jetsons: The Movie logo is a trademark of Universal City Studios, Inc.

Meet the Jetsons, a typical family of the future—George and Jane and their two children, Judy and Elroy. Astro is the family dog, but not just any dog. Astro can talk. Whenever he gives George a big slurpy kiss, he says, "I ruv you, Rorge!" And then there's Rosie, the Jetsons' robotic maid. Rosie solves every household problem with a wave of her control rod.

But even Rosie could not solve the problem of rush-hour traffic. One morning, George Jetson found himself stuck in his jetcar on the way to work.

"Okay," George said, eyeing the traffic. "It's time for the Jetson traffic-beater . . . Inflate-a-cop!"

George pushed a button, and immediately a rubber figure popped up and inflated on the seat beside him. Then he pulled a microphone from his dashboard and imitated the sound of a police siren. Cars pulled over and made way for George.

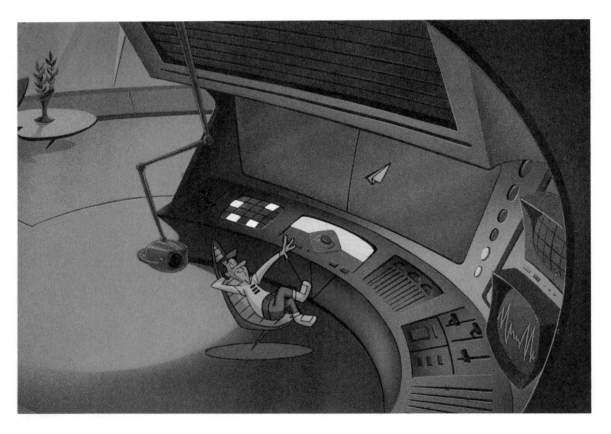

In just a few minutes George reached his office at Spacely Sprockets and Spindles. As he did every day, George pushed a large button on his desk, and instantly the computers started humming.

George felt very pleased with himself. "This is George Jetson," he said into his intercom. "I'm just reporting to say that whatever it is I do, I just did it again."

George picked up a paper airplane and sailed it around the office. Then he put his feet up on his desk and fell asleep.

Meanwhile, George's boss, Mr. Spacely, was bragging about the new factory he built in outer space to make sprockets. "My factory is simply out of this world!" he boasted. "I have the most incredible assembly line. It takes the rock from underground, removes metal from it, and turns the metal into my wonderful sprockets."

Scarcely were the words out of his mouth when a call came from Rudy 2, the robot who helped run the factory. "Mr. Spacely," Rudy said, "the assembly line has broken down again. And my boss has quit. That makes the fourth one!"

Mr. Spacely paced back and forth. "What'll I do?" he asked himself. "I need someone new to run the plant. Someone who's loyal to Spacely Sprockets. Someone who'll work for peanuts. Someone not too bright, and someone who can push a button."

Spacely put the information into his computer. A picture of George Jetson appeared on the screen.

"Jetson!" bellowed Spacely's voice from George's office wall screen. "You! Here! Now!"

In a flash, George was wide-awake and whooshing through the huge clear-plastic tube that carried people through the plant.

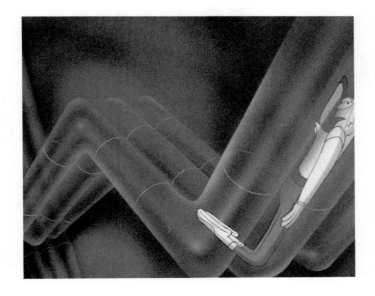

"Congratulations, Vice-President Jetson," said Mr. Spacely with a wide grin.

"Did you say 'vice-president'?" George replied in disbelief.

"Right. Vice-president in charge of the Spacely Sprocket and Spindle Orbiting Ore Asteroid Manufacturing Plant."

"Up—up there?" George stammered.

"Ah, how quickly you grasp things," said Spacely. "With your family beside you, you'll face a new challenge—space, the final frontier!"

When George arrived home that evening, he told everyone the news. "And we've got to move tomorrow!" he added.

Before the Jetsons knew it, they were packed and on their way. Everyone was excited except Judy, who was upset about having to leave her boyfriend behind.

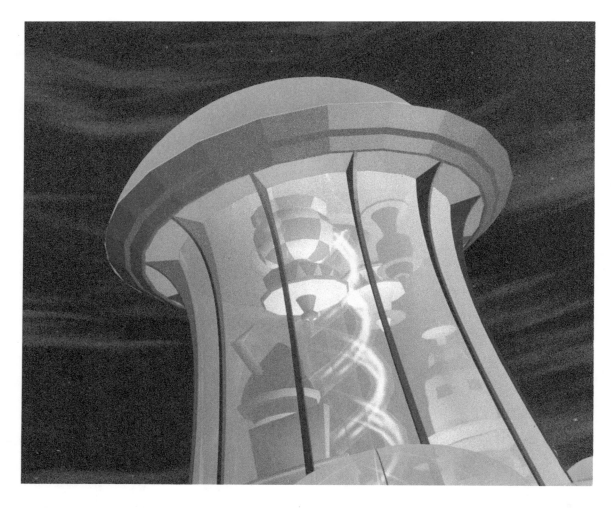

Soon the Jetsons flew by the space station that was connected to Spacely's asteroid. The station was like nothing they had ever seen before. In the center, under a huge clear plastic dome, was the Galaxy Galleria. It was a place where people met—a town square and a shopping mall rolled into one—with spectacular holographic scenery.

From the Galleria, transparent tubes stretched far away, like spokes of a wheel. On the end of every spoke hung a clear globe. Each globe was a suburb where people, robots, and space creatures lived and worked.

The Jetsons' new apartment in the InterGalactic Garden Estates was very much like their old one—except it was completely empty. Then Rosie clicked her control rod. Lights came on. Furniture sprang out from the walls. A kitchen rose up, and out of the oven came a freshly baked cake on which was written, "Welcome, Jetsons!"

That afternoon Elroy went out to explore the neighborhood. At dinnertime he returned with three furry blue creatures.

"I'm Bertie Furbelow," said the biggest creature. "Meet my wife, Gertie, and our daughter, Fergee. We're your next-door neighbors."

The Jetsons thought the Furbelows were a little strange, but they enjoyed meeting their new neighbors. And they were looking forward to many wonderful times in their new home.

The next day everybody gathered at the plant.

"And now, the moment we've all been waiting for," George announced proudly. He pushed the button, and the sprocket-making machinery started up. Everything went well—for a little while.

Suddenly there was a loud crash. Sprockets started to fly off the assembly line. Everyone ran for cover. Mr. Spacely, who was watching on a screen, was furious.

There was nothing George could do except shut down the plant.

That evening, Rudy 2, the plant foreman, came to George's apartment and spoke frankly. "George, since the plant opened, there's been an unusual number of...glitches. I thought we'd cleared them all up, but they keep happening. It may be safer for you to leave."

"And lose my chance to be a vice-president? No way!" George told him. "George Jetson doesn't run away from a glitch. We just need to make a few repairs tomorrow. Then the magic Jetson finger will show what it can do."

But the next morning the assembly line went haywire again. When George tried to see what was wrong, he got caught on it.

"Stop this crazy thing!" he yelled to Rudy.

"I can't!" Rudy yelled back. "It's stuck!"

George couldn't escape. He went right through the crating machine and wound up in a box with a sprocket on his nose.

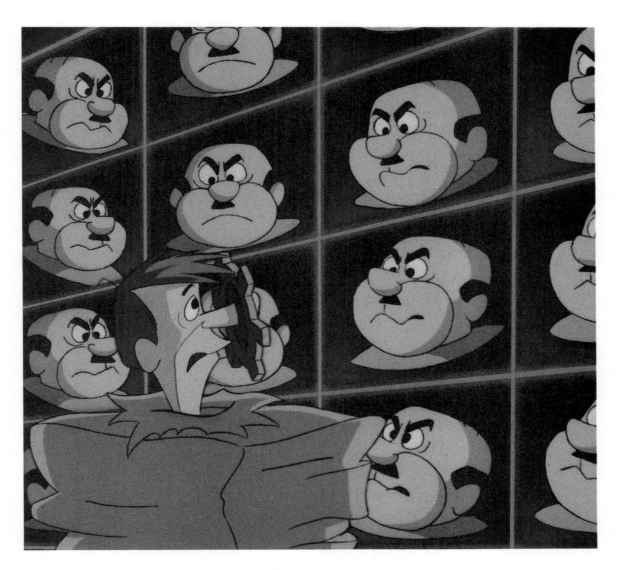

Dozens of angry Spacely faces appeared on the screen before him. "I think I know what the glitch is, Jetson!" the Spacelys roared. "I'm looking at him!"

Bruised and upset, George went home to rest. That night once again Rudy tried to convince George to leave. "Those aren't accidents," he said. "They are warnings."

"Well, I'm not leaving," said George. "Someone's sneaking in and fouling things up. I'm going back to keep watch."

That's just what George did. "All right, whoever you are," he announced bravely in the dark factory. "You've got George Jetson to deal with."

George waited for someone to strike, but no one came. And soon he fell fast asleep. It was then that little creatures called Grunchees stole out from their hiding places and carried George away to their underground city.

Luckily Rudy decided to check up on George. When he found no sign of George at the plant, he rushed to the Jetsons' home and reported George's disappearance to Jane.

"I'll tell Elroy," she said. But Elroy wasn't in his room.

"Oh, no!" Jane shouted. "Elroy's gone too! Come on, Astro. Let's get Judy and her new boyfriend, Apollo. They'll help us find George and Elroy!"

The rescue squad finally found George and Elroy in the Grunchees' underground town. Elroy had made an important discovery.

"Spacely's mining operation has been destroying the Grunchees' homes," he announced. "That's why they've been making the assembly line go crazy. Dad, you've got to shut down the factory!"

"You want me to do *what*?" George roared. "What about my job? No, no, no!"

Before George could say anything else, the ground began to shake. Dust and rocks fell all around. Now George understood what the plant was doing to the Grunchees' homes.

"Someone's started the assembly line again!" George yelled. "We've got to get out of here!"

At last everyone made their way safely up to the plant. Mr. Spacely was standing there. He had started the assembly line, and he had known all along about the Grunchees' homes.

"All you care about is money," George scolded.

Judy's boyfriend, Apollo, said, "Mr. Spacely, up here all different kinds of life forms work hard to get along."

"That's right," said George. "If you let the Grunchees run the plant, they'll find a way to protect their homes. And I'm sure they'll sell you sprockets at a fair price."

And so a deal was struck, and the Grunchees even found a way to recycle old sprockets from Earth. Their asteroid would not have to be destroyed. This meant that George was out of a job. The Jetsons had to pack up once again and move back to their old home. They were sad to leave, and there were long farewells.

As the Jetsons took off in their jetcar and began their journey through space, Elroy pointed and shouted, "Look, Dad! The Grunchees are on the roof of our apartment."

The Grunchees had spelled out a message in big blinking lights. It said, "Thanks, George!"